# Christmas Sins

## A Sins & Secrets Club Holiday Novella

# H. N. DeFore

ALL RIGHTS RESERVED. No portion of this book may be reproduced or transferred in any form or by any means, graphic, photocopying, recording, taping or by any other storage retrieval system, without express written permission from the authors, except for use of brief quotations in a book review.

This is a work of fiction. Similarities to real people, places, or events are entirely coincidental.

Copyright © 2024 H. N. DeFore.

Written by H. N. DeFore
Edited by Heather Knight-Burton
Cover design by H. N. DeFore

# Dedication

If your xmas gift isn't hard, ready, and eager to please, is it even a gift?

Happy (spicy) holidays.

# Also by H. N. DeFore

### Sins and Secrets Series
Terms of Obsession *Rules of Play * Applause (short story) * Lessons to Learn * Pleasure to Earn * Slice of Desire * Games of Temptation *

### What's Left Trilogy
What's Left of Me * What's Left of You * What's Left of Us

### Crossover Clubs Series
Lace & Sins

### Holidays & Hijinks Series
Christmas Side Hustle * Decking My Halls * Jingle in JulyMy Mile High * (newsletter) * Xing Out My Exes * New Me, Dead You * Bunny Hunting * Holidays & Hijinks Shorts

### Deadly Endings Series
Down from the Tower * Beneath Swan Lake

### Off Grid Billionaires
Arizona Vol. * Kentucky Vol. * Missouri Vol.

# TRIGGER WARNING LIST

<u>If no triggers, skip to Chapter 1.</u>

This is a dark romance story that can be read as a standalone novel. This novel does depict the following triggers:

Explicit kink play
Exhibitionism
Hand necklaces
Anal play
Bondage play
Fear of heights / risk play outdoors
Minor mentions pet play
Temperature play / ice play
Primal play / chase me
Obsessive men
And eager, possessive men who want to pleasure their partners

Please read with discretion.

# 1 Anita

As the only formally married person in my friend group, I'm the one who usually has holiday plans. I used to semi-force my friends to come over for Christmas dinner, and it mainly consisted of Myla making forced small talk with my ex-husband and Laci finding creative ways to throw bits of food at his head. It was always painstakingly uncomfortable, but I took pride in having anyone who actually wanted to spend the festivities with me. So I would get the tree done up in a lavish fashion, do my best to pretend things between myself and my ex were healthy and normal, and we all fake-grinned through the holiday.

Now? The Christmas tree Russell helped me put up a few days ago is twice as tall as anything Henry could stomach having in the house, and he told me to splurge and get one of those fancy, frosted, pre-lit trees. It's literally the centerpiece of the entire downstairs and I have no shame over that.

"God, I thought you were jolly before," Myla says, popping open another box of holiday decor. Just because the tree is done doesn't mean I'm finished with the house. I know this is possibly going to scare off my chipper boyfriend when he gets an eyeful of the amount of tinsel that's spilling onto the floor. The tree was one thing. This is everything else. Russell has no idea what he's agreed to.

*1*

"Was it necessary to pack every decoration you had and drag it to Russell's when you moved?" Laci asks, balanced precariously on the ladder that leads to a rather large attic. She's doing a fantastic job grabbing things and more or less lobbing them down on our heads, and her heels today are extra excessive with the white-and-red glitter. At least she's not playing Scrooge tonight in that outfit, and she's already claimed to have plans for later.

"It's *festive*," I correct, eyeing the box of extra-large ornaments. Laci found the decrepit tree I used to have at my old place, the one that Henry thought was more than enough and he never wanted to splurge on anything else. It looked a little less sad in the house I once shared with Henry, but maybe that's because my life there was a little sad in general. I've grown since then but the tree sure hasn't. I don't think I can even get it out of the box without the artificial branches falling apart. I thought it was extravagant until Russell spent real money on me and proved to me I was always settling with Henry.

Laci clicks her tongue, leaning into the attic once more. "Couldn't we wait for the guys to do this?"

"If you didn't drop all my ornaments down on our heads things would go better," I respond helpfully, digging around in the next box to find a Santa hat. Myla sticks out her tongue, taking out something sparkly to twine into her braids. The faux frosted branch glimmers against her dark hair. "At least try and be careful, Lace."

"You know what's festive," Laci chimes, climbing down the ladder, "a pole."

"We are *not* installing a stripper pole in here," I reply, heaving a sigh. I know Laci has some sort of secret dungeon over at Emilio's, but that's the kind of sight I don't want to see. She's already suggested we call it the North Pole and take Christmas pictures for my family in front of it.

The mortification is real. I still can't believe she suggested that. I don't think it's all that funny, but it's made Myla cackle a couple times.

"Gee Nita, relax. We all know you have a camera room for recording when you fuck," Myla replies, crossing her arms as she grins mischievously. "That's what, a step down from porn?"

Groaning, I pivot on my heel and head to the stairs. "Well, bah humbug to the both of you."

They giggle behind me, and I fight back the smile as I jog down the stairs, eyeing the bracelet Russell gave me a week ago.

Now that's a little much. It's not just a bracelet, it records. Invasive? Probably. But I suddenly have the ability to send Russell recordings from anywhere, and I might not have a true exhibition kink but I damn well enjoy teasing my boyfriend.

*Boyfriend*. He's shifted from being a Dom through the summer and early fall to my boyfriend. We're not talking marriage, but it feels serious. Too serious to bring up to the girls tonight before the party. Myla has a collar that's basically a wedding ring, and Emilio will more than likely stab anyone for looking at Laci wrong. It's all very *close* to wedded bliss without touching the subject, and we each have a different version of a serious relationship. Happiness found us each in just the right way.

My mind drifts to Serenity. I guess a daddy kink has to be on par with wedding bells somehow, right? Or maybe the thought hasn't even crossed her mind. Can't say I've asked her. The last few times we've talked it's all about the party tonight at the club, and the guys are way too excited for this to be just another night.

*Gift night.* That's what they called it. I kind of thought that meant everyone would bring a gift, but I've been told several times it's all about the gift we pick or are gifted. I have no idea what's in store, but Russell keeps making jokes about *Christmas Sins* and I've given up asking him what that even means. The gifts are provided by the club, we just need to show up.

"Do you think we need costumes?" Laci asks, coming up behind me to grab one of the mugs of hot chocolate I made earlier before bouncing off to the table. "Like slutty elves?"

"I think that's a little much," Myla replies, pausing beside me. I'm pretty sure Christmas is a touchy subject on her end, but all I know is last Christmas, David got her onstage to perform. How can this holiday be more extreme?

"The guys are supposed to be back soon," I say, changing subjects. "And then we head to the club."

"I need to change," Myla replies, eyeing her clothes. She came from the office, her Dom David dropping her off so he could go and take care of something before the party tonight.

"They said we'll like it," Laci calls from the table, and I glance over to see that she's using one of the chairs to prop up her feet. She looks the most relaxed out of the three of us. "I trust my Master. It's going to be fun."

"Trust isn't my concern," I grumble, thinking of the things my friends like. It's more showy, more in your face. I like my kinks, but I also prefer to stay behind doors or walls when I play at the club. I don't need an audience to enjoy myself. But Myla loves being watched, and Laci is without shame. I don't need to be that showy.

Hopefully we don't have to perform or something. I want to enjoy the holiday… whatever this is. It's not a showcase like years past at Sins and Secrets. Apparently this is an idea Callie came up with, and after some discussion, Emeric and Serenity went along with it.

If the managers of the club agreed, how bad can it possibly be?

My eyes widen when Russell guides me into the club a few hours later. It looks like Christmas threw up over the entranceway, and although I love it, I think Myla is quietly critiquing it behind me. She really isn't a festive person.

"I think Callie went overboard with the lights," Russell admits, the Christmas bulbs making his blonde hair a rainbow of colors as we enter. There's usually a sexy ambiance in the club to set the mood, but this is an entirely different vibe tonight.

There's still a sort of dress code, but it's definitely a holiday version of the usually fancy clothing all of the members wear. My holiday dress is nothing special compared to the flashy outfit Laci put on, and I'm glad Russell was only joking about wearing white sweats with a red stripe.

Sort of. They looked really hot, and I wouldn't mind seeing him in them around the house.

"Hoe, hoe, hoes!" Callie cries, jumping around the space. She appears to be tossing handfuls of candy canes at people, and she's got on a Santa hat and skirt. Her torso is naked, save for Christmas tree-shaped pasties covering her nipples. The thigh-highs are festive too and her make-up had one eye shadowed with green and the other with red.

"It's supposed to be ho, ho, ho," Serenity mutters, standing nearby beside Tyson. They make an odd pairing, like each is waiting on someone else. She blushes when Callie winks and starts up her chant again, skipping the other way. "That's not the kind of festivity I had in mind."

"Chill," Tyson tells her with a laugh, brushing back his hair. It's long and loose, and just makes me think about wrapping my fingers in it if he ever gets to join us again. "She's having fun. Besides, you're the one who gave her free reign."

"I suppose that was a mistake," Serenity mutters, touching her forehead as she turns. It's obvious she's worrying too much. Hopefully Emeric can calm her down when he arrives. "I'm going to just let her have her fun."

She wanders off, and my eyes find Nate. Callie's partner is also dressed in something close to a Santa outfit, though I think his Santa pants are of the tear-away variety from the buttons on each side, and I only see one Santa hat between the two of them. He's carrying around a sack of all things like a stereotypical Santa Clause, though I think most don't have washboard abs and they probably wear shirts.

I pause, turning to blink up at Russell. "What in the world is going on?"

He laughs, crossing an arm around me to hold me close. "It's gift night."

Shaking me head, a smile works it's way across my lips. They took gift night seriously.

His grin remains, and we pace towards the bar. They are talking to another couple before Nate opens up the sack he's carrying. I'm getting kinky Christmas déjà vu.

"That's the fun thing about the holidays," Russell says, and when I glance up at him, his eyes glint with mischief. He's wearing his lanyard and ID badge like normal, the only thing about the dress code that stayed the same, and he fiddles with it between his fingers. Easy access clothing is a theme tonight, which I suppose makes sense if everyone is here for gift night. "You never know what kind of gift Santa's going to give you."

My eyes widen. "Nate really is handing out gifts, isn't he? I didn't picture him to be the one doing that."

"I heard it's another one of Callie's ideas. It's a game of sins tonight."

Oh yeah, that definitely sounds like something Callie came up with. She starts up her chant again, and this time I can't stop smiling as she drags Nate around the room. The building is built with a loop, so you can usually go down either hall and end up back in the main entrance. But the far hallway is closed off tonight, making me all the more curious.

I'm certain people are playing further in the club, so it's a little different taking this long to get past the entranceway. Laci snags my attention as she tugs Emilio along, looking like she wants to come over to the bar. Unlike me she went for sexy even in the freezing weather, her heels clicking on the floor as she holds onto him. She gestures to us, and her moody partner just glances over without a smile.

I like Emilio, I really do. But he's just a little too cold for me.

Russell's fingers drag over the back of my neck, and I focus on him again. "Enjoy the night, Lifeline. The club will be closed for a couple days around Christmas, so we won't be able to come back for a little bit."

I frown, thinking about the calendar. I know Serenity blocked out four days for the holiday, which almost seems like a little much. While we aren't always at the club, I like knowing the option is there if we want to get out of the house. Then again, Christmas is my favorite time of the year so even if we can't come to the club on Christmas Eve tomorrow, I've already made plans of my own.

I'm certain Russell has, too, but he has yet to share with me what the rest of our holiday plans are for this year.

When my eyes find Myla again, she's standing beside the two Santas, frowning as she watches Callie talk animatedly. The boisterous blonde dropped her voice to speak with the couple, but it doesn't seem to help ease my friend's mood at all. Myla fidgets, even with David running his fingers up and down her spine. After a moment, Nate shifts towards them, opening the ridiculous sack he's been lugging around.

I guess she's going first.

# 2 David

Myla doesn't smile, even when Callie gives us a little shimmy and tries to liven the mood. Usually my partner loves to speak to the waitress, but right now nothing has lifted her spirits. She seemed a little off earlier when I swung by Russell's to pick her up, but right now her mood's spiraling to Scrooge levels.

Callie glares at me, apparently hoping there's something I can do to help. I've already tried to brighten her smile three times, but Myla keeps looking at me with a pinched frown. "Darling-"

"Don't darling me," Myla cuts in, and she pulls back from all three of us. Callie and Nate exchange a glance, and I watch the hesitation on his face as he debates closing the bag. They aren't going to force her to participate, but it's kind of the theme of the night.

Blowing out a breath, I grasp her hip and pull her close again to speak in her ear. Her spine straightens as I pull her against my chest, and even if the couple standing opposite us wouldn't care what I have to say I'd like to keep things private. "Be a good girl and reach into the bag. Play the game with me. If that's still not a good enough present for tonight we can go to New York and burn your mother's house down."

She snorts, but some of the tension leaves her body. I know this is because of her mother's chosen family, and it seems that Christmas is her most favorite time to contact her eldest daughter just to make a dig. Her mother better hope to God we never cross paths, because no one treats my girl like this. If her damn mom wasn't the culprit, I'd have already found a way to deal with this mess.

Myla clears her throat, looking at Callie and Nate again. "Okay, I'll take a present."

"That's the spirit," Callie says, clapping her hands as a grin spreads across her face. "Now, Santa knows you enjoy being watched, Myla."

We both glance towards Nate, who looks like he's trying hard to not burst out laughing. I wonder if this is the routine they plan on following with everyone who comes in. Myla clears her throat before she manages to utter a response. "Um, yes."

"We have a gift for that," Callie says knowingly, waving a hand. It makes her tits swing with every move, and even though I'm pretty sure Santa here is supposed to be in charge of the presents, this is Callie's show. "Let's see... good little exhibisionists can pick one of the blue boxes. Go!"

Myla blinks, glancing in my direction. There's half a dozen small blue boxes mixed into the bag, covered in either snowflakes or polka dots. I get the feeling Callie had a lot of fun setting up for tonight.

I shrug, and she reaches in to pick up a one covered in snowflakes. This game night is different from anything I've seen at the club before, so I can't say I have any idea what's going to happen next.

"Oh, you'll like that one," Callie says with a wink, crossing her arms. "Now open the box and follow the instructions."

"Instructions?" Myla glances my way once more. She makes it sound like homework instead of a gift.

"You'll see," Nate says, one side of his mouth lifting to a grin. "You'll have fun, trust me. A lot of thought went into tonight. Maybe too much."

"Oh, hush," Callie says, waving him off, her grin never wavering. "It's meant to be an experience. In fact, let's go piss off Emilio next," she continues, hooking her arm through Nate's to drag him off. "You two have fun!"

My gaze fixes on Myla again. She studies the small box, her hand hovering over the lid. There's nothing saying we can't open it up right here, so I gesture for her to go ahead. With a shrug, she pops the top off. Inside there's a small piece of paper and a thin bit of silk. She frowns as she pulls both items out before handing them to me.

I eye the paper. *Room 58* is written in the middle in a very feminine hand.

"What's that mean?" Myla asks, fingering my collar at her throat. The rose gold necklace gleams in the reflective Christmas lights, making it look multicolored.

I unwrap the silk next, and it's a long piece with the word *Eyes* printed on one side. Glancing at her, I grin.

"Looks like you're going in blind," I tell her,

twirling my finger. She frowns but spins, letting me place the blindfold over her eyes and secure it around her braids. There's no instruction on when to use the blindfold, but I imagine if it was for the spot we're going it would just be in there already.

"But how will I know people are watching?" she asks, a bit breathless. We've played this game plenty of times, but usually I set it up. This is new, and if Callie or Serenity planned it, which seems the most likely, who knows what we're in for.

Leaning in behind her, I let my breath ghost over her cheek. "You're going to have to trust me, darling. Don't worry, I'll be sure to give our audience a show."

She hums, some of the tension dropping from her shoulders, and I flatten the little paper box before sliding that and the paper into my pocket. I lace her arm through mine as we turn and walk down the hallway. So far as I can tell, at least right now, the stage is closed. But Julio and his group are down there, so maybe there's a show or demonstration coming up.

Myla's steps are sure as she walks with me, her faith in me unwavering. As we walk I notice that there are numbers above the private rooms as well as cases and sections of furniture down the long hallway. The numbers seem to be randomly placed, so I'm guessing they didn't want anyone to be able to figure out where their number leads.

"That's... creative?" Myla says after I tell her about it, but she sounds confused. I get that, because it looks like a lot of work for a single night.

Some of the rooms are already in use, and I see one or two groups down the hall as we walk. I maneuver her in front of me, guiding her along, and her breathing picks up the further we walk. I find our number halfway down the next curve of the hall, frowning as I look up at the label.

We stand for too long, and Myla squirms. "Sir?"

I click my tongue, guiding her forward. "Found our number."

The door opens easily and I eye the glass-walled space. It's cramped, and Myla immediately picks up on that as I help her in and press against her back, her hands pushing against the opposite side of the wall.

"Where are we?" she asks, breathless. There isn't a tremor in her body, but I can feel her unease. This is a tight spot, but I'll give it to Callie. It's creative.

I grasp Myla's arms, turning so she's faced down the narrow space enough to walk forward. The glass on one wall lets me study the people still walking by. "You know those window displays down the hallway where Rich started putting some of the new products for the store?"

Myla's steps falter as I lead her into the window display, the space just big enough to play around. The glass keeps us separated from anyone who would be foolish enough to try and join. Thankfully, the club is only open to experienced members tonight. Myla wants to be watched and admired and desired, but she'll freeze up and shut down if someone else so much as tries to touch her hair.

And I'd have to kill someone. It would be a bloody Christmas from that point on.

Her short heels wobble as she steps across the smooth surface, and her arms fly out to keep balance as her nervousness kicks in. Her fingertips are just a little too short to reach either side as she moves, so as far as she knows this space could be bigger. I let her feel her way to the chair in the center of the space, knowing the point of the blindfold is to deny her that sense. She desperately wants to see and be seen.

It's a kind of torture to make her wait, and my cock stiffens as I watch her fidget, lowering to the chair with my guiding hand when I move forward. My eyes leave her to look through the rest of the space, spotting another note on the door that I missed.

*Toys provided in the box. Christmas is the time of giving. Give your partner and her admirers what they desire.*

My eyes snap up, peering through the glass. Some people look up at us as they pass, and not all have a partner who is blindfolded. This seems to be done to go with Myla's exhibition kink.

No one is directly watching though, not like they paid for a show. I know there's people here who want my partner, it's part of the game. But security is pretty good at weeding out the problems, and no one dangerous is allowed within breathing distance of Myla. Not after everything that went on with her ex.

Keeping her blindfold in place, I grasp her braids and flip them over the back of the chair. She opens her mouth, hands sliding along the chair to try and get an idea of what's happening, but I grip her hair and tug her head back.

She gasps, willing to share her cries of pleasure with me and whoever is nearby. I study my collar on her neck for a moment, wondering when I should slide the matching ring on her finger, before my gaze drifts down. Her snug dress rode up while we walked and I love that it covers almost nothing. It's hot beneath the lights in the display window, and her throat bobs as she swallows and a single bead of sweat slides down from her hairline.

Without taking my eyes off her, I palm her breasts over the dress. Her little whimpers break through the silence until she is all I can hear, see, and think of. I pinch at her nipples until they harden beneath the fabric, before shifting my stance so I can kick her legs open.

She helps, pushing her thighs wide so she's bare to anyone watching. Unlike the first time I fucked her in the club, she's unashamed that people could see up her dress or her bare pussy as I undress her. I lean over, staring at how wet she looks even from here. The thrill of what's next keeps her on edge, and she has no idea who could be watching.

"Are you going to be good for me or fight," I ask her, dragging my hand down her braids before I release the hold on her hair. Tapping one thigh as I walk by, I eye the large box on the opposite side of the chair. "Keep those spread for me."

Myla whimpers as I open the box and study the supplies. There's more than enough here to work with, and I wonder how many times I can get her to cum in this window before she's exhausted.

My fingers close over the handle of a leather paddle. I could fuck her with this, make her fuck the toys before I ever give her what she wants. As much as I enjoy watching her cum, I like making her work for it too.

I select what I need from the box, turning back to find her legs bouncing impatiently as she waits. I like the tension working through her as she tilts her head back and forth, trying to figure out what'll happen next. We've walked through the club enough times for her to know the window displays I'm talking about, so I wonder how she envisions the space looking if we're in here.

Flipping the roll of tape in my hand, I move back and stand in front of her. No one will be able to see her like this but it isn't part of the show. Not yet. This is a gift for her, just like one of the items I just pulled from that box.

In my free hand, I run the hard end of the cane along her thigh, making her jump at the contact. Someone painted it white and red like a candy cane, so it's fitting with the rest of the night. "Relax, darling. Be good while I get you ready."

"For?" her voice comes out needy, a little breathless, and we haven't started yet.

I grin to myself, eyeing the top of the cane. This will be so useful in a minute. As much as I like impact play, Myla needs soft impact - like leather wrapped whips and my hand. Canes or anything hard will set her off, but she isn't panicking as I trail the cane up the other thigh, sliding it between her parted legs. She trusts me.

"Up," I tell her, and she's quick to follow when the pressure of the cane disappears. I help her slide out of the tight dress, deciding to opt for removal over warmth. There's little else on her, and she works like a doll as I strip off the bra and panties until she's completely bare to the eyes outside. A few people look as they pass, but we're all here for our own gifts tonight.

I take her hand, guiding her to the glass and adjust the eye cover once there. The rest of the toys lay on the floor as I take her hands, pressing them flat to the glass.

"David-"

"What?" I taunt, opening the tape. She jumps at the noise, but doesn't fight when I press the black sex tape over one hand then the other to keep her in place. It's not the purpose I would normally use it for, but her blindfold is otherwise sufficient until we're ready.

Leaning in, I lick a trail down her neck, the braids keeping her lovely locks from getting in the way. "Stay still, darling. And I'll make you see the stars you love again."

# 3 Myla

*The stars you love again.*

David's words wash over me as the blindfold remains in place, and I know he's talking about the first time we were together on the roof. It's far too cold right now to chance going outside to do anything like that, but if he makes me cum hard enough, the stars will swim in my vision.

And I love it.

He finishes prepping, leaving me to nothing but the sounds of him setting up and my own pounding heart. He said we're in one of the window displays? They're usually stuffed with shelves and mannequins showcasing the latest outfits in stock in Rich's store. So they obviously had to clean out the areas before the gift night started, because I haven't run into much of anything.

All at once my nerves come alive, feeling David running something solid along my pussy like he did with my thighs. I'm already soaked, pulling against the tape that's got my hands locked in place, and the hard object is stiffer than a dildo and not silky like a cock.

I swallow hard when he moves the item up and it just keeps grazing my clit. Again, and again, and again…

"Is that the cane?" I choke out.

His chuckle is low, right by my ear, and the sound shoots right to my clit. "Oh, it's a special cane. There's a tag on it. I'll show you when we're done. It seems to be a gift."

I don't have time to question him on that. Suddenly, the cane isn't just a blunt object. It slides back down my body to click against the floor, before a buzzing sound fills the room like an echo.

I'm so tightly coiled from the tension and teasing, when the vibrating toy pushes against my clit my knees buckle. I grunt loudly, bowing my back to push as hard against the device as I can, and David's arm wraps around my middle and holds me in place as he tortures me.

"Such a good girl," he growls. "Cum for me."

His hips aren't touching me, and I feel him shifting but can't determine how. His arm stays locked around me as the toy goes, making my legs tremble as he keeps me in place.

He growls when I start rocking, seeking so much more from the toy than it can give. My body is barely listening to my mind as it melts, my breasts aching with as much need as my pussy as I rock against the narrow tip of the cane, needing more.

When David presses his cock against my entrance from behind I almost weep with appreciation. Once he fills me, I know between the little buzzing toy and the feel of him that I'm going to come with a nice, loud scream.

As he slides in, one of his hands yanks the blindfold off, the sudden light blinding me as he shoves inside me and makes my brain turn off in one smooth motion.

The thrust shoves me forward, making my hard nipples graze the glass. I cry out, still adjusting to my senses, and as I blink I realize there are people watching us.

My eyes peer around and I feel David slowly pulling back. Distantly I know my focus should be on him. But I see some faces I recognize and some I don't, all of whom either glance or stare as they pass.

I sputter when David slams deep again, my gaze locking on Anita and Russell as they pass. My friend looks horrified and turns away, and she often turns a blind eye to us at the club if we're in the middle of something she would rather not see. But Russell eyes us, looking not only at me but David behind me as he snaps his hips forward again and makes me cry out. Before they are too far out of sight, Russell shoots me a smirk and wink, before turning back to a blushing Anita and guiding her away.

"See how taboo you look?" David growls, his voice more gravely and deep when he's fucking me. I whimper as the toy continues to buzz, finally dropping my gaze from the audience to the toy torturing my clit.

It's definitely the cane, but I'm at a loss on how it stands. Neither of David's hands hold it in place, and my legs are spread too far and it's not touching the glass. Nothing obvious holds it in place, making my whole body hum with overstimulation.

David snakes an arm around us, his hand coming to lock around my throat just above his collar. He flexes his hand as he thrusts into me, my body shaking so much I'm not sure I'll be able to bear my weight the entire time. He applies pressure as I moan, his fingers clenching over my neck. "Look at the stars, darling."

I scream, the sound bouncing back in our little display. My neck snaps backward, bumping his chest, and I stare up at the ceiling as David picks up speed. People could be cheering us on for all I fucking care at this point. The vibrating cane is making my eyes water in the best way. I can't see David, I can't arch that far, but he presses closer behind me and I vaguely hear the cane fall. The little buzzing sound dimly fills the space, but between the sounds of our skin slapping together and our panting breaths I can barely hear it.

"Good girl," he says, tugging so I follow the pull of his hand. I'm lightheaded when we straighten up, his cock buried as deep as it'll go inside me, and I blink for a moment before focusing out the glass again and trying to find my balance without the cane pressed to my clit.

I know people are watching. But all I want to do is cum on my Sir's cock again, and see if he can wring another orgasm or two out of me.

He shoves forward, one arm coming up to cup my breast before we're smashed against the glass, his cock pounding furiously into my pussy as he edges closer. The smooth rhythm of his movements turns to a frenzy, and I grind back against him as he teases first one then the other nipple, pushing his hand between me and the glass.

His tongue is on me, finding my neck, and he licks the sweat-slicked skin before he bites down. I whimper, bucking like mad against his body. I won't last much longer, and neither will he.

When he releases my skin, the spot is sensitive and tingling. "Good girl. I'm going to worship and own every piece of you, Myla."

Between the command in his tone and the power of his body as his cock continues to plunge into me, it's too much. I shatter, screaming as my head drops forward against the glass, my eyes misting when the orgasm sweeps through me. It's almost too much all at once.

David pumps into me for a few more strokes before pulling out, and one hand tears the tape free that's covering my right hand. I'm only vaguely aware until he turns me, his other hand coming to gather then grip both of my braids. My other hand is still taped too high on the glass to get to my knees.

Our eyes meet, the same possessive adoration shining in his iris that's always there. "Tongue."

Obediently I stick my tongue out, holding his gaze. I know exactly what he wants, and I soften my gaze as he fists his cock, staring directly at my face as he jerks himself.

"Fuck," he grunts, and after a few moments I taste his cum. Without dropping my gaze to look I don't see the mess he's making, but I do feel where the sticky cum lands on my breasts and neck, painting me in his orgasm.

The moment he's finished he groans,

reaching around me and freeing my other hand. I slump against him, mess and all, and David wastes no time wrapping his arms around me and lifting me, moving us back from the glass. My body feels like it's floating, riding high, and I don't even look to see if anyone's still watching us.

I don't know where it came from, but David kicks a pillow behind the lone chair and sets me down on the floor, a blanket already spread haphazardly. I take in the details slowly, like I'm watching a movie, and he sets me down and kisses my temple.

"Water," he says, reaching behind me. I partially roll, glancing at what he's doing, and find a large box. Probably a stock box with supplies. He digs out a water bottle and a candy cane of all things, handing both to me. "I'll draw the curtain."

"Curtain?"

He winks, pushing off the ground, and it's then that I realize he lost his tie and jacket, but he's still got his now stained pants and his shirt, though that's unbuttoned with the sleeves rolled up. He maintained most of his clothes while he stripped me down, and the reality brings a smile to my face as I crack open the water.

That man always manages to make me smile.

I'm surprised when he pulls at a cord and a curtain falls over the window, hiding us from view. It really is a tight space, and someone with claustrophobia would probably have a fit. But it's just the right size for us plus the supplies, and a silly grin paints my lips as I realize there's still sex tape stuck to the glass.

David bends, picking up the cane, and it's only then that I realize the toy was still buzzing. He presses something I can't see and the room goes silent, before crossing back to me and propping the cane against the chair.

There really is a gift tag tied to one end. I squint at it as I unwrap the candy cane, David coming to sit beside me. He's still breathing heavily, but he's brought back his own water and guzzles down half before looking towards me.

I nod to the cane, the candy-cane design really making it festive. "What's the tag say?"

David snorts as I scoot closer until I can nuzzle against him, his legs kicking out so I can lay in his lap. It's relaxing here, and when he combs his fingers through my hair that calming subspace feeling settles over me.

"I imagine Callie wrote it," he says, barely keeping my focus. "It says 'have fun you hoe, hoe, hoes'."

"She's milking that one," I say, but it's with a smile. I eye the cane, fighting the urge to close my eyes for just a moment. "Are there words on the candy cane?"

"Oh yeah," he snorts. "Again, a Callie idea. I think the bosses really gave her some liberties this year."

"Oh?" I say, my eyes drifting closed. David's calming touch keeps working through my hair, and after a moment I feel something soft dancing across my skin. He's wiping me off, and I can't believe I momentarily forgot about the mess. I've gotten so accustomed to him taking care of me, knowing what I need after he's rough, that I sometimes forget what he needs too.

When I don't feel sticky anymore I push his hand away, flipping my braids and rolling a little so he can see the collar on my throat. *His* collar. The one he proudly shared with me, the one that marks us as a couple both in and outside of the club.

His fingers trace along the heart before he speaks. His tone is gentle even as the words make me snort. "It's another pun. 'The North Pole always finds the right hole'."

# 4 Emilio

"I definitely saw them," Laci says, fidgeting with her Santa hat. It's a little ironic that Mr. and Mrs. Claus are prancing around with a Santa sack and she dressed up like Santa too, just a pink version.

Honestly, after listening to the amount of decor that Anita owns, I'm kind of glad that Laci's holiday addiction is focused on her Christmas outfit, not how many Christmas lights she can hang up around the house. She did comment at the beginning of the month that if I didn't offer some type of input she'd put up what she wants.

I should've listened. The pink Christmas tree glowing in my front window made Russell burst out laughing the last time he was over, and it was kind of satisfying to punch him in the arm for it. At least Laci limits how much decor she puts up.

Still…

"Does it need to be pink?" I ask, staring at the hat again. At one point she had a traditional red Santa hat, but somewhere along the way it became pink before we drove over here, just like the striped thigh highs and her pretty dress. She's more done-up than her friends and we both know that's how she likes it.

"It needed to match," Laci defends, raising an eyebrow. She did some intricate makeup for tonight, and I smirk and run my fingers along her jaw as we stand near a few of the shelves that haven't been emptied, watching the two Santas wander around and give people gifts.

I tried to wander back towards my room, and got smacked in the head by Callie. We are not allowed to go back to play, even to my private fucking room, until we've gotten a gift.

"I've never gotten a gift at a sex club before," Laci goes on, tapping her chin. She's baiting me, I know she is, and she flutters her lashes like she doesn't mean anything by the jab. "Do we have to declare naughty or nice?"

"Pet," I grunt, watching her smile turn mischievous as she tries my patience, "I have no idea what the plan is."

Laci grins, turning until she has space and kneels on the floor. I like her like that, on her knees and eager. I didn't bring a leash for her tonight, mostly because she keeps mentioning wanting a new one. Laci isn't the subtle type, and if she wants something she'll say so. We haven't added to our collection at home recently, and I know the shop is open here at the club. Maybe we'll buy a souvenir for Christmas on the way out.

As she kneels, I can't help tracing her face with my finger. Her lips pout the longer I keep her waiting, her eyes narrowing just as hair as we stare at each other. I'm going to enjoy punishing the bratty side of her later, and if she really wants to be defiant we still have the St. Andrews Cross at the house. Maybe I'll let her scream out her wishes for the holidays while I turn her ass red.

I think she senses my dirty thoughts,

nipping at my finger when it passes across her lips again. I growl, ready to play, when Callie shimmies up with a tired looking Nate.

He gives me a rueful smile and beckons to his partner, who bows with a flourish. "Ready for your present?"

"I knew there would be a present!" Laci says, jumping to her feet. Bright eyes peer up at me, and I wonder what she's hoping for. "Can I pick?"

"Oh, yours is different," Callie says, shaking a finger at us. She meets my gaze, winks, and continues on. "Your Master has a private room. We laid out a gift to unwrap in there. Perhaps you should pick a leash for the walk and go enjoy yourselves."

Nate stands to one side, looking between her and the sack. I wonder why he's hauling that thing around if they only need it for certain attendees. It's no wonder that mall Santa's just sit there; it looks like that thing is heavy.

Laci spins, eager eyes peering at me, and it's time to play. Callie winks before waving and wandering off. She talked to David and Myla for a couple minutes, so I'm curious what awaits us if she so quickly admitted that the gift is already in the room.

Slowly, she sinks to her knees, wide eyes staring up at me. "Master."

I nod and she bows her head. Her long hair falls forward, free and loose around her face. Her submission so early makes my cock twitch, and I wonder how good my pet will be tonight.

Her Barbie side is the girl I left outside in the car, cracking jokes and getting excited about the holiday even if she tried to play it cool. Inside the club Laci is my good little pet, and I'll walk her back to the room with a leash on to degrade her just a little bit. She'll eat it up.

"The dress. Lose it," I tell her, my voice commanding. She keeps her head bowed, undoing the buttons on the front with ease as I turn. There's a row of leashes hung nearby, and I wonder how many people will be using them tonight.

All of them are a little too on the nose for me, covered in Christmas decor or snowflakes or something wintery. I pick one that's decorated with lights and turn back, finding Laci without her dress, still wearing the see-through underwear I picked out earlier today. She gives me a cocky grin as she drops the dress to one side and crosses her arms, challenging me.

*Fucking brat.* She makes a game out of my patience sometimes. As much as she wants to crawl around on the floor and be my pet, she's naturally full of attitude and all about pushing my buttons.

I raise a brow, beckoning her closer. We're turning to our roles now and if she doesn't think I'm going to turn her ass red for being so defiant before I fuck it, she's sorely mistaken.

Instead of coming over, she slides her legs together, drops her hands to the floor, and bows her head. "Master, I just want to see the room already."

A smile tries to pull at my lips and I push it down. She's so gift-driven tonight it's almost cute if it didn't border on bratty. I step closer, scooping her dress up once I reach her, and loop the collar around her neck before tightening the leather. I know some might abuse the strength of the leash, choking their partner, but if anyone invited to the Christmas party tried something like that the club would ban them.

I push her hair out of the way, and she looks up at me with longing in her eyes before I step away. Tugging at the leash, she follows the command and stays on her knees despite the harsh floor, crawling behind me as we take the familiar path to the private room I pay for.

The thing about the private rooms is people don't traditionally go in there. I clean the space, keep the toys and the area sanitized, and although security can have access if needed (as is required) no one ever comes in to intervene. Laci is the only woman to be in this room with me, ever, and our trust in each other is unwavering. She knows secrets about me that no one else does.

Laci moves quickly despite crawling, and she's gotten used to the process when we're in the club. Usually she crawls to a seat in the theater before a performance, but this is different. It's more tile to crawl over, and I glance back as we move. A lot of the members who came in tonight are already in the middle of play, and as I look around I notice numbers all over the place.

My door appears before the display

windows down the hallway, and by then Laci's back is starting to curl. Her knees are hurting, and those heels will be pulling on her ankles and poking her ass from moving around. But we both know she likes a little punishment with her degradation, and if she was too uncomfortable she'd speak up.

I punch in the code, holding the door for her to move ahead of me. She's not as fast as before, and even with the curtain of hair covering her face I think I see her wince. I didn't think I did anything out of the ordinary having her crawl, but maybe the cold from outside left her skin extra tender.

Once the door closes, I drop her leash and scoop her up, enjoying the little gasp that slips from her lips. "There's my sweet pet. Let's get you up on the bed."

Laci smiles when I place her on the mattress, her back sinking into the comfortable bedding. It's not fluffed up like at home with all the pillows she's brought into my house, but it is comfortable. Her eyes close briefly as she enjoys the comfort, and I eye her knees.

One of the thigh highs is torn. There's a cut on her kneecap, and I grind my teeth as I skim my fingers across the spot. A little bit of blood dried to the mark and against the fabric of her sock, and her eyes pop open again as I inspect it. "That's sensitive."

"And how did it happen?" I ask, surfing through my memory. She didn't mention anything so I assumed she could crawl all the way back here just fine. We would've just walked if she spoke up.

Laci shrugs against the sheets. "Broken ornaments are sharp. I was dropping boxes out of Anita's attic and accidentally dropped one when no one was watching. I went to pick up the pieces and sliced my knee on a clear one. Who has clear ornaments?"

I raise a brow, listening to her chatter as I undo the straps of her shoes. They slide off both legs, and I pull the thigh highs next. Crawling around irritated the spot and that's just another reason she should communicate her hurts with me. I ball up the fabric, tossing it towards the waste bin near the door, and she props herself up on her elbows. "I liked that set."

"It's trash now," I say, ignoring the way she frowns. "You tell me when you're hurt, Laci."

She scoffs, but her body falls down into the sheets again when I trail my hands up her legs. "It's a scratch."

"A cut. And crawling like my pet hurt you. You tell me where it hurts, and it's my job to make it better. You keep it a secret, I can only make it worse."

Laci's head tilts against the pillows, curious eyes watching me. Her hands slide down her body until she cups her pussy, drawing her legs up a bit to bend her knees. "And if I say it hurts here?"

My eyes flash, propping my hands on either side of her body. "Show me."

She wiggles out of the thong that's absolutely soaked, and I toss it somewhere near her dress behind us. Her legs fall open again, and she uses two fingers to spread her bare pussy lips so I can see all of her. "Inside. There's an ache. Maybe your tongue will fix it."

I eye her. Tasting her is something I enjoy, but it's already deviating from any plans I have. I'm supposed to have her in here so I can check out whatever the gift -

My thoughts cut off, and I peer around. So where is the gift?

"Milo?" Laci says, her voice a little wobbly. "Everything okay?"

"We're missing a present," I say, but she shoots me a smirk. "What?"

Laci points her finger, raising a brow. "Up."

I glance up, my reflection staring down at me. The wall of mirrors in here is one of Laci's favorite things, even if it gets dangerous sometimes. But the mirror above is different. There used to be just one. Now there's several, spread across the ceiling so no matter where I fuck her in this room I can make her stare at the ceiling and watch the whole thing.

My cock hardens at the idea.

"Not a bad gift," I mutter, wondering how they pulled this off. I thought the gift was supposed to be the experience, but those mirrors look expensive.

Laci whimpers, and I watch her in the glass above us. Her legs come up, knees pressing together, and she squirms on the bed. She's horny watching herself, and when her eyes drift to me in the mirror, I grin.

This will be fun.

Leaning forward, I drop my gaze and shove apart her thighs. She's eager, falling back into the pillows once more as I tug her down the bed, looking up at her as I run my tongue up and down her entrance.

She moans, lifting her hips. I do it twice more, teasing her. Her fingers scratch at the sheets, and I lift my eyes to stay on her face as I slide my tongue inside her.

"Master..."

Her voice is breathy as I play with her, keeping her spread with one hand while the other teases at her ass. She loves when I take her there, and if she thinks it'll be any different tonight with the new additions hanging above us she's wrong. I could turn her, put her on her hands and knees, and she could watch us in the wall of mirrors across from the bed while I stare up at her, the mirrors on the ceiling giving almost a full-circle view of us.

"There," she whimpers, chest rising from the bed when I tease her ass. There's no lube, and although she's good at opening up for me, hurting her isn't on my agenda. She studies me with hooded eyes, trying to twist her fingers into the short lengths of my dark hair. I narrow my gaze on her, letting my teeth graze her sensitive lips.

"Fuck," she continues, dropping to the bed again. Her body rocks against my face, and I know she wants everything I'll give before I go back to being her Master. I shift my hand so I can tease both her holes at once, and she rocks hard against me.

I hum against her pussy lips, and she cums fast with a sudden cry. I know how to tip her over the edge after all this time, and her pleased cries echo in the mirrored room as I lap up all of her.

After a moment I kiss her entrance, pulling back as she pants. Her hands have fisted the sheets, pulling them out of place, and without all of her clothes she's deliciously bare for me.

I glance at the ceiling, appreciating the aerial view. "We're doing the photoshoot for Christmas Eve."

Laci giggles, knowing what I'm talking about. There's a specific outfit back at the house that I got for her to wear, and I intend on taking all the pictures of her in it that I need before I shred it off her body. It's going to be my favorite Christmas so far. I can already feel it.

She lifts to her elbows, chest still heaving. Without a word she puckers her lips, tilting her head as she waits for me.

But I'm not just going to give in to her tonight. "Ask?"

She flutters her lashes again. "Kiss?"

I lean in, letting her taste herself on my tongue. She offers a contented sigh, melting into the kiss as our dances dance together. I give her a moment to enjoy before pulling back, twirling my fingers before I step away. "Roll over. Hands and knees."

"Am I going to be punished now, Master?"

"If you keep behaving like a brat instead of a

pet you might be."

Laci laughs, but I hear her shifting around as I collect what I need. When I turn back she's in the position I asked for, wavy hair tossed to one side to hang over her shoulder with her face turned towards me, watching.

"Little pets obey," I remind her, watching as I approach. She's taken the liberty of removing her bra, leaving her utterly naked in the mirrored room. I'm still fully dressed, putting her at a disadvantage when I return with a few items. There isn't much in my hands, and there doesn't need to be. I plan on fucking her, not toying with her.

Her eyes rake over me, searching for all the things I'm not holding. When I rub my hands together, everything I collected hidden from view, her eyes narrow. "What did you grab?"

"Oh, my pet, where's the fun in telling you that? Be a good girl and stare ahead. I'll make you feel good, right after you take your punishment."

# 5 Laci

It takes a lot of self control to not let my attitude slip through and try Emilio's patience. He's a good Master, with far too much tolerance for all the brattiness I throw at him, but right now I do want to try and be good. He's already irked about the cut on my knee, but pressed against the mattress it's barely a dull throb. He might be slightly overreacting about me not mentioning that.

Even though I know he wants me to. He always wants to know what's bothering me, so he can kiss away the hurt. He's done that more times than he needs to, and even if he had some issues of his own in the past he's done a lot of healing in the last year. Now, he's a little overprotective at times but in the best way. I've never had a guy care this much for me before.

The hard pressure of his hand connecting with my ass makes me jolt on the bed, and the sheets barely bother the stupid cut in my knee. I don't have time to think about the sting of pain anywhere on my body before he's striking the other cheek. My breath hitches as he continues the pattern, alternating the strength of his spankings from harsh to light, giving my skin almost no time to recover.

I gasp and moan beneath him, wishing he would give me something more to stave off the ache in my cheeks.

"Eyes ahead," he commands, and I snap my

gaze to the wall across from us. Milo likes to be able to see all things at all times, so it's no surprise that his penetrating dark eyes are staring directly into mine across the small room. He watches the way my jaw falls open when his hand connects when my ass again, and I'm trembling each time he adds another spank. I know I gave him hell in the hallway, but he's going to turn my ass into a cherry before he even fucks me.

A few strikes later he eases up, using both palms to massage the sensitive skin. I whimper at the contact, balling my hands against the sheets, and try to stop the tremors from dancing through my body. That made me way too horny and way too sensitive. He's toying with me.

I cry out and jump at the feel of something cold dripping down my ass crack. My head snaps back, leaving Emilio's dark gaze behind as I stare up at the ceiling. Above I can see his hands flexing behind me, his fingers working to kneed my tender skin. I can't quite tell what he's brought over from this angle, but he promised not to toy with me…

One hand leaves my ass and I turn to peer over my shoulder, trying to see what he's doing. His eyes narrow on me as he removes an item from his pocket of all things, fiddling with it where I can't see. I'm about to make a snarky comment when he lifts the item, pouring the cool liquid over my ass again.

I moan at the contact. It's lube, so he's going to fuck my ass tonight. My hands tighten on the sheets, thinking of how good the burn will feel.

Emilio used to work with me to get his cock to fit inside my ass, but now we've done this so often that gentleness is barely needed anymore.

He wastes no time, his hands losing their grip on me and abandoning my burning cheeks. One finger probes at my asshole, and all I can do is let my head hang forward as I moan. I love this part.

There's a dull noise, and I shriek when that fingertip shoves deep inside me at the same time a toy clamps over my clit. It applies pressure like suction, and I can barely manage a strangled cry as the sudden, violent orgasm hits me at the two different sensations.

The toy stays in place, his hand coming to grip my hair. "Watch us, pet. Watch and see how pretty you look coming on my cock."

I force my eyes to not roll at his words, eyeing our reflection as he adds a second finger in one hard stroke, the tip of another already eagerly working through the lube to press against my hole. I lick my lips, his powerful body tense all over as he fights the urge to fuck me, his intense eyes focused on the task at hand.

When the third pushes in, I can't take it anymore. "God, Emilio, just fuck me! Fuck me nice and hard, Master. Pretty, pretty please."

I've resorted to begging, but the reward is well worth it when I feel his fingers leave my desperate body, the toy still working to keep me sensitive. I rock backward, searching for more, and then there's the smooth feel of the head of his cock brushing my skin. His hands grab my reddened ass, making me whimper as he parts my ass and spreads me open, his slick cock coming to rest against my asshole.

He pushes forward without warning, the head of his cock popping inside me with no resistance now that he's coated in lube. I moan loudly at the feel of his thick cock working its way inside me, and I wiggle enough that he releases my hair so I fall forward on the bed. My hands grip the sheets, and when he gives one hard shove forward until he's balls deep inside me all I can do is tear the sheets out of place, my back arching with pleasure.

"You do love it when I take any hole I want," Milo grunts, his grip coming to rest on each hip. I can't lift up again as he shifts, halfway pinning me to the mattress with his body as he fucks me.

"Yes!" The toy still torturing my clit leaves no room to argue, and I feel my legs starting to shake before I can stop them. He's fucked me upside down on the Saint Andrews cross at home, but this... this is something else.

"And you're going to let me fuck you however many times I want," he continues, and I can hear the challenge in his voice. Does he think I'll tap out after one round? "I'll win this fight, pet. Endurance is my strength."

"And pettiness is mine," I gasp as his hips slam into me a little harder. I'm trying his patience as I wiggle back against him, the toy on my clit begging me to cum again.

He lets go of my ass on one side to smack it, hard. I cum from the feeling, because I'm already so worked up there's no fighting it. I turn into his little rag doll as he fucks me, a willing pet that just wants to serve.

Milo gets me submissive like this when it comes to sex. He's the only person I'll ever relinquish this much control to.

"Cum again," he growls, and I slam my hips back against his trying to chase the next orgasm. If he's telling me to finish, he's getting close too.

Just before I cum, a hand shoots out and squeezes my throat. I see stars when the orgasm sweeps through me, making everything feel all that more intense. His cock slides all the way inside me as he stills, the warmth of him filling my ass as he finishes inside me.

I sigh, letting the last bits of tension in my body drain away as his hand slowly loosens, massaging the same spot he just dripped on my neck. It feels so good, and I sink into his grip as he slowly works his way back out of me. The little toy on my clit never relents, so by the time he's free I'm a shaking mess all over again. I feel his hands guiding me down, and until the sheets press into one side I don't even realize that I've leaned to one side.

His fingers touch my clit and I whimper, my legs jerking wildly at the oversensitized touch. His chuckle is low as he works the toy free, and when it's no longer wringing orgasms out of me I slump deeper into the bed.

"There you go, pet," he tells me, pulling at the sheets to part way cover me. Without the heat of his body I realize it's a little bit chilly in here, or maybe it's just the sweat that's cooling over my skin. "Let's look at this knee now."

"It's a scrape," I grumble, throwing one arm over my eyes. I've tried to help clean up after sex in the past, and for the most part it just seems to irritate Milo. He wants to check me over and care for me after we're finished, cleaning me up and ensuring I munch on something after that much exercise. Who am I to tell him no?

"You know, pet," he says after a moment, and I shift my arm around enough to crack one eye open and watch him. He shakes a bottle of water at me, and after a moment I hold out my other arm and take it. "I planned to have you crawl back to the car, but we can't be doing that on the asphalt in the parking lot with a cut on your knee."

I open my eyes wider. We don't usually play outside of the walls of the club, not unless we're home. It's always an in-the-club type of deal. Milo is deadly protective, and he's killed for me before. It's not typically worth the risk of him pulling his gun on someone to do something in the parking lot or even parked outside the house.

"Guess we'll have to improvise," he continues, holding out a hand for me to sit up. I snap the seal on the water once he lets go, guzzling down half of it. "You can sit at my feet instead."

My pussy buzzes at the idea, and I knew he

couldn't possibly be done with me yet. At this rate we're going to fuck on the side of the road before we make it back to his place and throw caution straight to hell. "In here?"

"Of course not," he says, smirking when I look up again. My hand lifts to play with his stubble, and he turns to kiss my wrist before continuing. "In the theater. Looks like you have something new to wear."

"Oh?" I sit up straighter. Clothes are my everything, even if Milo usually takes mine off. I didn't see him bring a package in here, so maybe it was hidden already.

He holds up a finger, stepping away. The room has just enough storage to house whatever Milo has personally paid for to keep in this private room, plus any of the freebies offered to every member. He stops by the small storage cabinet, picking up a box and turning to me.

"It's pink!" I squeal, tossing the bottle aside as I reach for the box. He hands it over, the pink ribbon pale around the white box. "I thought we were doing gifts at home."

"It's not from me," he says with a shrug. "It's to both of us."

I pause long enough to eye the tag, the girly handwriting giving me a good idea who wrote this: *For One of Santa's Good Little Reindeers.*

"This is another Callie idea isn't it?" I say, even as I tear at the ribbon. Milo chuckles as I do all the unwrapping.

"She's running this holiday," he agrees,

taking a step back when I toss tissue paper at him to find my gift.

I grin wide, holding up the outfit. It's soft, being made out of leather, and there are two parts. The first is a brown bralette that's missing the cups so it resembles a harness. The crotchless shorts match the top and both are trimmed in pink.

"I think it's a reindeer," I say, wiggling my brows at Milo. He has a bemused smile on his face, and after I dig out the thigh high socks I discover there's nothing else in the box. "She didn't pack an outfit for you though."

"If Callie planned this, she's not going to try to dress me," he replies, taking the box away. "Let's see it then, pet."

I grin. It's amazing how good Callie did picking my size. I almost wonder if she had help, but then again that woman sees so many bodies she's probably pretty damn good at guessing. When I spin around so Milo can see all of me instead of just watching in the mirrors, his gaze hungrily glides over me.

Holding up the final item, I wiggle my eyebrows at him. "It came with a pink nose. Does that mean I can pretend to be Vixen?"

Emilio growls, walking up to me to toss the shiny nose away. It's possibly some kind of toy, but now it's too far out of reach to be sure. His arms slide around me, pressing my body to his, and my still sensitive slit thrives at the pressure all over again. His knee presses up, and I wrap my arms around his neck.

I wet my lips, fluttering my lashes obnoxiously until his lips lift into a grin. "I can take a little pain, Master, promise. If you want me on my knees I'll be such a good girl."

"You're always my little *vixen*, Laci," he admits, leaning forward to kiss my lips. It's a softer, gentler version from moments ago when he was devouring me. "Now, get on your knees if you're going to be so stubborn. Those socks should help along the way, but you know you have a word to get it to stop. After all, little pet, good girls crawl."

# 6 Serenity

Despite the Christmas gift party being prominently led by Callie, I'm still a nervous mess wandering around making sure everything is going okay.

There's a shibari demonstration going on now in the theater, which is kind of a group gift for a few of the couples. Some have assigned spaces to receive their gifts and some are luck of the draw. It's far too many possibilities for my mind to handle, and I'm seriously glad Callie decided to spearhead this idea since I'm pretty burnt out on what to do to make the night special.

Gifts with a twist. If this goes well, Jo and Vinny might approve to make this a yearly deal. I'm not too sure what they think; since it's Callie's deal, she's the one chatting with them about it.

"Are you having any fun yet, Ms. Serenity?"

I almost jump out of my skin at the voice. I got lost in my own thoughts as I wander around, constantly shooing Callie and Nate away despite their determination to pass along my gift. Once Emeric gets a hold of me I'm finished working for the night, and there's just so much to do. I haven't seen him in a little while, but hopefully that means things are going okay and he's just wandering around.

But I didn't expect to see Rich here. He beams at me as I turn to face him, his shirt and jeans dark and dashing as normal. Every time I've seen this man, he's dressed to blend in. I guess owning the shop that Sins & Secrets features in-house comes with the territory. He's here to show off products, not himself.

Studying Rich now, I realize I've never specifically paid attention to his features. Pale blond hair blends with pale skin, and I get the feeling Rich is sold to his work. The vivid purple eyes that stare back at me are startling, and for a moment I think they are contacts. Minus the bizarre eye color he looks almost like old Victorian, or a snobby blond haired wizard.

Rich chuckles, drawing me from my thoughts. "I've got a message for you."

My eyebrows lift, and on instinct I look around for Callie and Nate. They appear to be talking to Anita and Russell at the moment, so I guess I won't have to try and dodge them yet. "Me?"

Rich nods, smirking as he pulls out a box. My jaw drops as he winks at me. "Emeric handed me that. Looks like he already picked a present for you."

"What..." My voice trails off as Callie turns and spots us. She winks too and gives me a shimmy, puckering her lips to blow me a kiss before Nate distracts her again. She turns back, leaving me dumbfounded. "He's already picked?"

"I suppose he thought you would avoid the two Santas since you already know the procedure for tonight," he says, smiling before his eyes drift past me. The smile falls almost immediately, and I glance over my shoulder to follow his gaze.

*What is her name...*

Kimber. Her name slides into place as she jogs out of the front doors, her face blotchy and red. She's carrying a pair of boots, and I'm only slightly surprised she didn't leave those at the door. Judging from the hunch of her shoulders and the red eyes I'd say she's upset.

"I'll let you go find your gift," Rich says, drawing my attention again. I've barely turned my head before he's moving past, and I blink as he walks off without a word. I track him for a moment, noting that he walks down the same path Kimber did towards the front doors.

*Interesting.*

I move towards the nearest chair. The crowd's thinned out and most are off enjoying their gifts. It gives me a moment of peace, and I take a breath before popping open the green and gold box. Inside there's...

Frowning, I pull out the metal ring. It's just a ring, nothing specifically sticking out. The silver ring is almost wide enough to fit around my wrist, so maybe it's a bracelet?

That feels... lackluster. I saw some of the gifts for tonight and they were absolutely amazing. Still, there's a small note in the box. Emeric must've set this up after selecting the box because it's in his familiar script:

*To the roof, little one.*

My eyes widen, my gaze snapping towards

the stairs that lead to the roof. Why on earth would he be up there, I wonder.

I swallow hard. There are so many reasons he would want to go up there, if I'm being honest. Maybe I should stop thinking so much.

One more glance around the room, and I know that Callie and Nate have it covered. I can hear her calling *"hoe, hoe, hoe!"* again and I know for the time being no one is looking for me.

I almost go up to the office to double-check things, but once I go up there I know I won't come back down. I'll try to avoid the roof and figure out the ring-bracelet thing on my own. Instead I bolster my courage and remind myself that Daddy always has my interests in mind, so there must be a reason for freezing my ass off in December on the rooftop. Pivoting, I hurry towards the stairs and rush outside. The cold steals my breath for a moment, forcing me to pause and take in the scenery.

The roof is surprisingly clear of ice, and I realize the maintenance team must handle this part of the club, too. I don't really think of the rooftop since I don't come up here, but I know that the members that do are always happy with what they find. There's a fire pit that's glowing and some vacant chairs, but no other members up here tonight. We closed the rooftop for the season, so we won't be disturbed up here.

I spot Emeric immediately, a beanie thrown over his shaggy hair and his chest missing a shirt. I almost scoff at that until he turns, the thick gray sweats he's wearing doing nothing to hide the outline of his erection. I pace quickly across the rooftop, the cold air making my teeth chatter. His dark eyes lock on me and once I'm close enough to touch, he drags me against him.

I grit my teeth when my hands land on his skin. "How are you warmer than me?"

He grins, sparkling white teeth catching the firelight. "Fire, doe eyes. Now, let's see what Santa brought you."

The ring is still clutched in my hand, and I shove it in his direction before I wrap my arms around myself. I went for a hot and sophisticated look tonight, the red dress offering a high slit that shows off my garters and adds sex appeal to my almost business-casual look. I had a Santa hat at one point, but Callie pouted that there were already two, and since this is her jam I took it off and fluffed up my hair instead.

Now, I really wish I kept the hat.

"Don't look so afraid, little one," Emeric taunts, one arm still corded around my back. "I'll warm you up real good."

"We have to do it out here?" I ask breathlessly. It's so cold I can feel it sinking deep into my skin. December in Denver is hit or miss with the weather, and, even though we rarely have a white Christmas, it's cold and sometimes icy for the better part of the month.

Emeric chuckles, tossing the ring in his hand. I still don't understand what the purpose is until he starts to twist his hand over the fire, warming the metal without dropping it in.

I tilt my head, my heartbeat slamming in my chest. "You aren't planning on branding me or something, are you?"

He quirks an eyebrow, but continues to twirl his hand over the flames. It's not going to turn the metal red hot, but it is going to make it warm, especially in the cold night out here. "I don't need to put a brand on you, little one. You're already marked by me in every way."

My cheeks heat. He's painted me with his cum more times than I can count, and we both know he makes a habit of coating me so I can wear him around when we're at the house or even sometimes when we're working. I don't let him get away with it at the club as often. Too many of the members can tell what's going on, and it's way too embarrassing on my end to admit I'm covered in his cum while walking the floor. I get that no one finds it that bizarre at a sex club, but it's still something I'm not totally adjusted to. Not to mention anytime he bites or sucks my skin hard enough to leave behind a mark. I like that version of marking even better.

"We're going to do something different for your gift," he continues, pulling back his hand. He's kept his fist closed, and when he drags his knuckles up my bare arm I shiver. He's so much warmer than I am right now. "I plotted with Callie. All your presents are already up here."

"Doesn't that ruin the fun?"

Emeric leans in, his nose brushing against mine. "I intended on doing something like this to you anyway. The Christmas party is just an excuse.

I've had this in mind for a while."

"And... what is it?"

One side of his mouth quirks up, and in nothing but the mood lighting and the fire he looks a little devilish. My fingers itch to brush his dark hair behind an ear, but I can't quite break the hold his penetrating green eyes have on me. "Go to the edge of the roof and I'll show you, little one."

I gape, staring at him. This is a four-story building, including the "basement" area that's really just the ground floor where the dungeon is indoors. It's only accessible from one side of the parking lot, and usually only staff is allowed through that entrance. Going to the edge while it's freezing while there might still be ice on the ground someplace -

"You're worrying," he tells me, grabbing my shoulder to spin me around. "That way. See the lights? Walk over there for me."

It's on the tip of my tongue to ask if he means crawl, but one look at the frozen concrete has me retracting the question. I'll tear my knees up out here if I don't manage to give myself frostbite while I'm at it. Emeric does some dirty things to me but bloody, primal play isn't for me.

I hurry across the cold ground, only slipping once, and when I reach the ledge I peer over the roof to the parking lot below. We sectioned off the parking for tonight since it's a smaller crowd and the bit of snow we did get had to be shoveled somewhere. A whole section of the parking lot is dark, but I swear I see something moving in the shadows. Two somethings in fact -

I shriek before a hand settles over my lips, something colder than the air outside sliding up my dress. I squirm against Emeric's hold as he leans into me, his toned chest cooling against my back. It's nothing though compared to whatever is climbing up my thigh, forcing my legs apart until they shake.

"I've shown you heat," he tells me, speaking into my ear, "and sensory deprivation, loss of sight and control. Now I'm going to show you cold and test your ability to be silent."

There's no time to ask what that means. The cold pushes up against my pussy, and he groans in my ear when there's no resistance. I swallow, both loving and hating my decision to forgo my underwear tonight.

"No thong?" he teases, and the cold presses against my pussy lips. I gasp, the ice definitely feeling wide and rounded like the head of a cock, and I lean back into him to try and peer up at his face.

"Is that…" my voice trails, and his dark chuckle fills the night.

"What, little one? Did you just realize Daddy is going to fuck you with an ice dick while you plead for a Christmas miracle?"

The ice slips inside me, and I press my lips together to stifle the cry. My whole body seizes up at the feel, lost in whether I love it or fear it.

Emeric slides the ice deeper, and it's not painful like I always pictured. Being fucked with ice always sounded like inserting frostbite into my body, but this is smooth and wet like the water you find in a chilled glass. It slides easily into my body, making me whimper as he pushes the frozen toy deeper and deeper inside me. My legs slide apart at their own accord, wanting to feel the toy deeper as I rock back against him. An icy gust of wind whips past, heightening my senses, and he licks a wet trail up my neck that cools along with the air.

My head lolls back, lost in the feel. It's criminal that ice can feel this good.

When he starts sliding the ice toy in and out of me, I can't stop the cry that escapes. So much for being quiet. He holds me against his chest as he fucks me with it, my moans spilling from my lips into the night. I peer up at the sky, watching the stars as the ice makes my pussy throb. I never expected it to feel this good.

"We're just getting started," he says with a chuckle, speaking into my ear. He keeps sliding the ice inside me, making me shake at the contact, and the whole time he never releases his grip on me. I'm just starting to get into it, the size of the icy toy dwindling the longer he plays with me, when he abruptly withdraws the toy.

Emeric shoves me forward, and I brace my hands on the edge of the building as a puff of breath leaves me. It's hard enough catching my breath when he plays, but up here I can't seem to grasp anything. Not my breath, a handhold, good footing -

His leg kicks mine wider apart, and I brace my hands on the cold stone beneath my palms.

He's not wrong, temperature can heighten the senses, but I love having things stolen from me too. I wiggle my ass backwards, seeking him, and even when I find his hard dick and start rocking again he doesn't mirror the movements. It goes on like this for a moment, and I ease up wondering if I've done something to upset him.

"Emeric-"

"Shh," he says, and then I feel the cold tingle of metal on my lips. I open my mouth to question it, and the ring slides into my mouth behind my teeth, forcing my mouth open. I trace the shape with my tongue experimentally. There's something attached to the sides that I can't quite place. "I'm going to fuck you, and you're going to do your best to silence those screams. When you can't anymore, you'll scream into the night for me, little one. Got it?"

I nod, the ring foreign in my mouth as he pulls tight, and I realize he must've used something to turn it into a sort of gag. The ring keeps my mouth open while the ties secure it to my head.

Emeric kisses my cheek when he's finished, his hands coming to rest on either side of mine. They've turned cold as I held still, my palms resting on the stone, and now with his arms surrounding mine I realize how chilly I am. "You can slap either of my hands twice if you want to stop, little one. Otherwise, you'll take Daddy's dick up here on the roof, understood?"

Nodding, I can feel my pussy clench at the idea. There's absolutely no way I can keep quiet for long, and we both know it. But with the ring in my mouth, it's also taken away the ability to hide my cries. I suppose that's deprivation of a different form.

"Words, Serenity," he growls, nipping at my neck. I jump at the contact, the graze of his teeth much more intense against my cold skin. "Say 'yes, Daddy' for me."

I swallow, the movement feeling strange with my mouth held open. "Yesh, Dabby."

It comes out garbled, but Emeric doesn't seem to mind. I barely catch his "*good girl*" when the wind picks up again, and the next moment I feel his cock against my ass as he lifts the skirt. I brace my hands on the stone ledge, fear and lust warring with each other as I stare at the dark pavement below.

But I have utter faith in my Daddy. He's never going to let me fall. As he braces an arm around my form, his cock sliding into place behind me, I know this is going to be a gift only he can give.

# 7 Emeric

Serenity lasts all of thirty seconds before she screams, the sound echoing off the buildings nearby. I grin against the curve of her throat, brushing more long blonde hair out of my way to lick down her neck again.

She vibrates with energy as I slide my cock inside her to the hilt, her head snapping back to press against my shoulder. She's up on her toes, unbalanced, and she whimpers as I still inside her. "Good girl."

Serenity whimpers, eyes closing against the starlight. The top of the building is fairly dark, the surrounding structures closed down as the holiday approaches. This is a unique opportunity to have her all to myself outdoors, when the area is otherwise closed to the club.

I hook a finger into the ring settled in her mouth, grinning at the idea Callie gave me when she was busy wrapping five-dozen boxes. Fixing the ring gag to work outside was a little tedious, but it did keep her guessing. Just like the ice dildo that Rich dropped off for me. I didn't have a good spot to store that, and I didn't want anything to happen to it while I was getting ready.

Now? It can melt under the lights for all I care.

Serenity moans as I snap my hips forward, picking a fast pace that leaves her squirming and panting. Pressing one palm to her lower stomach is going to bust my knuckles at this rate, but it keeps her from slamming painfully into the frozen stone. I want her to shiver with pleasure, not pain.

She must be swallowing her cries, because she manages to not make too much noise for several moments. I briefly spot movement down below, which might be the reason she's trying to suppress her moans. I can hear it in the way she catches each whimper, the metal ring offering little resistance to her cries. Her hands grip onto the wall like a vise, and her whole body is buzzing.

But I can almost see that beautiful brain going into overdrive, overthinking and over worrying about who might be in the parking lot. As if the security tonight would let a single member get hurt. We have the staff on rotation so anyone who wants to play can, while keeping everyone here safe and secure.

I grasp her shoulder, pushing her forward so she's flat to the stone instead of balancing on her hands over it. A gasp rings out in the night like music to my ears, but she's just too tense to relax into the moment. And I refuse to not make her cum at least a few times while we're out here. I have no idea when the rooftop will be exclusively available yet empty again.

Kissing the shell of her ear, she whimpers and rocks her hips back into me. "Think you have the energy to take me for a ride, little one?"

She shivers, and I'm not sure if it's from me or the cold. "Yes, Daddy."

Something about her breathy voice, the little

tremble to her words when her teeth chatter, makes my cock harder. I moan behind her, which just makes her bounce harder against me, before I press her to my body to keep still, and slowly pull out.

Serenity makes this whining noise that shouldn't sound as sexy as it does, and I spin us in one smooth motion so I'm the one against the wall. It isn't a full length wall, only coming up to her stomach, and it presses to my lower back. I lean back as I let her go, halfway propping myself up on the wall. My legs are long enough they still touch the ground, and that's what she studies first before peering over my shoulder.

"Go on," I tell her, gripping her thighs. I'm balanced, and there's no ice on the ledge to worry about. "If you ride me hard and fast we won't go over the edge."

Despite her shiver, she sends me a grin as she settles on top of me, her hand fisting my cock. The other grips my shoulder for balance, an uneasy breath leaving her as she peers over the edge.

I like to take risks. She has risks of her own, but this is a little outside both of our comfort zones. Still, she doesn't hesitate as she rubs the head of my cock against her dripping pussy, before slamming herself down my dick. The barbell piercing at my tip makes everything twice as sensitive as she slides her body down me, and I can't help but groan. "Fuck."

Her nails dig into my shoulder, the cool air outside making my nipples pebble as much as hers do. Even through the thin bra she wore today, and the flimsy dress, I can see each hardened peak. If I didn't need to keep us balanced so we don't fall off the roof my hands would be all over her.

She leans in, her tongue licking around the metal ring. She can't speak very well like that, and the way her brows crease for a moment I can tell she's desperate to be able to say something. I love her screams, and denying her voice is a different sort of deprivation.

I moan as she begins to move, shifting to dig my hands into the edge to keep us balanced. Her movements are frantic, the hand on my shoulder cold, but my skin is on fire every time she slams herself down my cock and makes us moan together. Her breathy little whimpers are a song I can hear even through the wind, and I tilt my head back and moan into the night.

Serenity whimpers, leaning forward to swirl her tongue against mine, tracing the piercing through my tongue with hers. She starts to move faster, her opposite hand gripping the edge right next to mine, and she whines again.

I look back at her, watching the lust swirl in her gaze. "Cum on me, gorgeous. Show me how beautiful you look in the night."

Her eyes are unfocused and I doubt she understands how gorgeous she looks against the white clouds and barely visible moon, her blonde hair catching in the wind to fan around us. She's like my personal north star, one I'll always follow home.

Serenity cries out, her nails shifting from my shoulder to my neck, and she screams through the metal ring. I'm not sure what words she says, but it all blends together as her body shakes on top of mine. I let go of the edge with one hand, holding her hip as I fuck up into her body while she rides the high.

It only takes me a few more strokes of pumping into her before I feel my cock twitch and explode, throwing my head back as the orgasm shoots through me, chasing hers. My hand stays firm on her hip, holding us together as she slowly comes down from the ride.

When the trembling subsides a little bit and turns to shivers, I know the cold is taking over. My chest is covered in a thin sheen of sweat that's quickly cooling and starting to freeze. I help her shift off of me, a moan slipping from her lips when my cock slides free from her pussy. I set her boot covered feet back on the ground, adjusting her dress so she's covered again.

My limbs are stiff with cold as I stand up straight, fixing the gray sweats. Her hands are already moving to remove the gag, and I reach up to help her undo the tie and pull the ring out of her mouth. My hand catches her jaw almost immediately, soothing her tired face with gentle pressure. "You did so good, little one."

Her eyes meet mine, hazy and sated even in the poor lighting. I keep one hand under her jaw, gently kissing her lips, and she groans as I pull away. "I d-don't think I ever keep my jaw o-open that long."

I nod, immediately gathering the few things we need and turning us towards the door. Serenity snuggles into my side, though I'm not sure how much warmer my skin is than hers. We make quick work across the rooftop, the wind stealing our words as we hurry for the door. It opens easily despite the weather, and I gently push her forward inside the heated building before stepping halfway in, propping the door open with my body.

"Emeric," she warns, wrapping her arms around herself. In the lights of the stairs I study her, reaching behind for the blanket I brought up here. Her eyes widen at the fluffy plaid thing, but she all but disappears beneath the blanket as I wrap it around her, taking my shirt next and sliding it back over my frozen skin. "Emeric, close the door. It's too cold."

I grin, nodding to the roof. "I know, Serenity. I wanted us to be up here."

She subtly rubs her thighs together, surely thinking about the game we just played. "So we could freeze while you teased me?"

"Hardly," I reply, winking as I turn to the service panel box in the wall. It requires a key that's tucked into my sweats, and I pop the door open and flip the switch.

I think she believes I'm turning off the rooftop lights, and I'll do that soon enough. But this is on a timer now that it's on, and I want her to see it up close.

Lights fill the rooftop, most strung on the canopy across the way and a good distance from the dying fire. I almost forgot about it, and I'll have to walk back out in a minute and throw snow on the dying embers. But with the low glow of the flames, she can see every visible light from the door.

"Stars?" she asks, focusing where I knew she would. The tremble in her voice is gone, possibly from warming up, but I think it's from awe more than anything. She's distracted from the cold.

Across the side opposite where we were, string lights glow against the otherwise bleak landscape. The mountains in the distance are shrouded by the low white clouds, giving the stars an ethereal glow against the dark buildings. Among all the small twinkling lights there's one a little larger, hung above the others. It's as high as I could go on the roof before it was advised as dangerous. The canopy and the privacy screens are already iffy with the fire department.

But the one star I placed is the one I hoped she'd see. I reach out, pulling her against me, and kiss the side of her jaw again. "Callie and Nate's gift is sexual. They gave you the ring gag."

She cuts a glance up to me, leaning away from my chest for a moment. "My jaw feels like it's going to fall off. My tongue is so damn dry from the wind. Maybe it's a gift to not be used outside in the middle of winter."

I chuckle, leaning in to kiss her again. She doesn't protest, and I'll get her whatever she pleases downstairs. "You'll get used to it, doe eyes.

I'll have you using it a lot from this point on. But that's not my gift."

Her eyes drift to the stars again, and I lean in to kiss her cheek and let the door fall closed a little bit more. I want to savor the moment before we go back downstairs. "You're my north star, little one. Wherever you go, that's where I find home."

# 8 Russell

Bracing my hands on either side of Anita, she blows out a steadying breath as she follows along with the routine Julio sets for the shibari class. We do plenty of this at home in our spare time (and sometimes during our working hours if I can talk her into being extra naughty) but she hasn't ever attended classes at the club. I've tried, Emeric's encouraged, but Anita still suffers from body-image issues from time to time.

I have never had an issue with her body. I love every curvy inch of her.

Her head whips around when Julio begins clapping, the girls who travel with him all joining in to congratulate the people who attended the class. The one couple who participated in the demonstrations, this was their gift of the night, but we are just in here passing the time. Callie cornered me before tonight even began, bombarding my phone with messages about waiting until the right time.

We don't want to freak out some of the members. Primal is a little hard for some to get into, and we don't need anyone panicking and making a call because they think things are getting out of hand with a little chasing.

"Do you think Callie is ready with our gift?" Anita asks, letting me help her out of the harness. It was an informative class, mostly the discussions of suspension and a few lifts. I can string Anita up much better at home without anyone's watchful eyes using my own personal setup.

I glance towards the doors, knowing it's getting late. Some couples have already finished. I'm betting Myla and David are all done by now. Anita blushed so pretty when we passed them earlier, but since they picked out one of the exhibition gifts, I had no idea where they would even be until we walked by. I have a decent idea what's coming tonight, since Callie asked me about it prior to deciding what kind of gift to plan for us.

Kissing Anita's cheek, I hope I've picked right. I very rarely doubt my decisions with her, but this one might push too far.

"Should be soon," I say, helping her down from the stage as she shakes out her shoulders. I haven't strung her up in over a week, and this just reminds me it's time to do it again.

Anita tugs on my arm, and I glance down at her. "Alpha?"

I thin my lips. Unless we're in the middle of play she never addresses me that way. Maybe she's getting nervous because we've been here so long and haven't accepted a gift. It's the whole point of the evening.

Or I suppose it could be the lesson, since Anita doesn't like to perform. But we were in a group, not singled out, and I kissed and touched her every single time she looked uncomfortable. She never requested that we stop, either.

"Don't fret, Lifeline," I tell her, winking. She scoffs, but there's a playful smile that slides across her lips. "They save the best for last."

"In random sex gifts?" she questions, sounding unconvinced.

Before I can respond Callie appears in the doorway to the theater. She tugs Nate along behind her, and I get the feeling my poor friend is just about finished with this game tonight. His steps are slower than before and he's no longer hiking the bag high up on his shoulder. Knowing the two of them, she'll make it up to him in time for playing along. I point at them instead of responding, and Anita pivots on her heel and takes a deep breath.

I lean forward, resting my chin on her shoulder as they approach. "Remember, all gifts come with a safeword."

She glances back, confusion marring her pretty features before Callie reaches out and grabs her hand. The Santa hat she had on earlier in the night is gone, and Nate's missing everything above the belt. At least the sack looks just about empty, so they have to be finishing up for the night. "Hoe, hoe, hoes!"

"I'm kind of amazed you've kept that up all night," I tell her, and she grins before looking at Nate. He shrugs, opens up the bag, and instead of asking Anita to grab something from inside, Callie leans over, shuffles something around, and pops out with a pretty red box. The white ribbon is a little squished from being in there so long but it's still wrapped well.

"Santa gives everyone the chance at a good time," Callie says, smirking at us as she hands over the gift. She looks a little tired but her smile is still genuine and happy. One pasty is starting to pull away from her skin, and as she talks Nate reaches out and smoothes the coverage back over her nipple piercing. "This one's a fun one, Anita. I promise. And if not I'll let you chase me sometime to make up for it."

Anita blinks, looking completely lost, and I snort at the joke. Instead of explaining, Callie leans in, kissing her on the cheek, grinning when she pulls back. "If that's out of your comfort zone I'll let you embarrass me sometime to make up for that, too. Now Mrs. Claus needs to get laid for doing all of the work for Santa."

"You did all the work because you were having fun," Nate corrects, but Anita is still staring at Callie with wide eyes. I asked her once if she'd ever want our third person during sex to be a girl, and she said no. Callie might be confusing her all over again without meaning to.

Callie winks, gesturing to the box before she turns. "You two have fun."

They leave the theater as quickly as they arrived, and Anita turns back as she tightly grips the present. "Did Callie just kiss me?"

"That's pretty tame for Callie," I remind her, and she blows out a breath. Anita dressed festively like her friends, the green dress and tights making me want to devour her. Julio's demonstration for shibari didn't include stripping, so I didn't get a tease of skin while we bided our time. "Why don't you open that?"

She looks down at the present like she's afraid. Most gifts tonight are small, but this one is large and rectangular and I happen to know what's inside. Callie just asked for the size, which I secretly found out at home without asking and now have memorized. I like to know everything about my girl.

Anita tugs off the ribbon, and I help her balance the box while we stand so she can take off the lid. Normally we couldn't just stand in the middle of the room like this, but nothing else will happen tonight. I've already seen Em and Laci sneak in and out of the theater, staying in the shadows so Anita didn't feel self conscious while they did… whatever they were doing. It was too dark where they sat for me to care.

She gasps as she opens the box, and I stare down at Callie's pick. The black boots have a slight heel but excellent traction, just like I told her to buy. They also look fur lined, so I don't have to worry about her getting too cold outside. Anita's confused gaze lifts to me, and I shoot her a wink. "Why don't you put those on?"

"Why do I have boots?" she asks, looking down at the heels she wore. There's nothing wrong with those, but she slipped in the parking lot on the way in. I have zero faith that she won't smack her face on the pavement outside running away from me, so different shoes are required for our gift.

I grab the nearest chair, dragging it out, and help her sit down. "Shoes. Off. You're wearing these."

"Why do I need boots?" she questions again, but she doesn't fight me as I push her to sit and slide her feet out of the heels. A little whine sticks in her throat when I massage the soles of her feet, and she wiggles around like she can't decide if it feels really good or if it tickles too much.

"Because the last thing I want to worry about when we're outside is your feet," I tell her, pulling out the boots. They fit like a glove, and I'm kind of amazed how well Callie did with the pick. Once they're on she stands, looking at me expectantly. "We're going down to the dungeon. It'll be cleared out by now."

Worry creases her brow. "Russell... you know I don't like dungeon play."

"You don't have to like it to run through it," I reply, watching as the worry turns to surprise. "There's an emergency exit door at the far end. The alarm on the door is disabled for tonight. We're going to go on a run."

Now the concern is gone, and her eyelids lower a little at the idea. She might not ask for it often, but I know from our last adventure in Rocky Mountain National Park that she enjoys being chased. "We aren't going to use any of the equipment down there?"

I chuckle low in my throat, leaning in to press my forehead to hers. "No, Lifeline. I don't need any of that to absolutely wreck you. I'd rather chase you and fuck you as my prize."

She bites her lip at the possessive note in my voice, and I rarely treat her like an absolute fuck toy but tonight I'm feeling like she deserves something more. The night in the park is still one of her favorites and even if I can't top it, I'd like to get close.

"You're going to chase me in the dungeon," she echoes, like she needs to repeat what I've said to understand. "Around all the toys?"

"And out the door," I go on, pacing after her. She walks backward to keep her eyes on me, and it's a good thing there aren't as many people in the club. No one stands in her way as we move, even as we reach the doorway. "I'll give you a head start, but then you're mine."

Her eyes flash before she glances down at the shoes. "I thought I was getting a sweet Christmas gift."

"You are," I tell her, the corner of my mouth quirking up. "But I'm more of a Krampus than jolly ol' Saint Nick. Your gift will be as dirty as you are."

Anita's eyes flash, and she pivots on the ball of her foot. We've managed to walk out of the theater, back into the main entrance of the club, and although we have to walk the long way around to get to the entrance of the dungeons, that doesn't deter me. My gaze stays locked on her, and after realizing she can't go the quick way she licks her lips, eyeing me through her lashes. "Catch me if you can, Alpha."

Something inside me growls at the challenge, but all I shoot her is a grin as she turns and half-runs away, mindful of the smooth and slippery floor. I count down in my head, staring after her, and my cock twitches where it's pressed beneath my waistband. I was already hard before, watching her in the class. Just because there wasn't a strip tease doesn't mean my lifeline wasn't sexy in a harness suspended above my face.

I cut my countdown short by two, because I physically cannot wait to sink into her. Waiting until the end of the night means a long teasing period, and to be honest I've been hanging on the idea of chasing Anita through the dungeon and the dark parking lot since Callie first told me the idea. It wasn't just a little box, it was specific to us, and as good as Callie is she wouldn't want to gift something that could trigger. From what I've seen tonight she's done an amazing job.

I don't look around as I pace to the dungeon's entrance. I vaguely realize the window display where David and Myla were earlier is dark, and the halls aren't crowded anymore. It's easy to maneuver around, and I spot a couple of the staff setting things in order again. All of it shifts to background noise as I search for my lifeline, and I find the entrance to the dungeon guarded for once. There's security usually around Sins and Secrets, but I suppose for the holiday event they had some extra precautions.

When I reach the chambers where dungeon play takes place, it's empty. I've never seen the space so quiet except before we open. It almost looks like nothings been touched tonight, which will help make it obvious where Anita has and hasn't been if she knocks anything over.

I take a moment to listen, to see if I can pick up on any heavy breathing. I've never brought Anita down here before, and it occurs to me that was a mistake. Pushing her too far is something I refuse to do.

But the room is silent. I've seen her panic, and there's no way she would stay this quiet. She could be a good little hider though. Maybe she learned something from our last adventure at the park. There's a few toys that aren't perfectly lined up, and one of the chains is on the floor instead of hung up. Maybe she ran through a display and took a couple things out on the way.

I creep around the room, ignoring the wall of toys and the open cages that I can see right through. There's nowhere to hide over there, and aside from a Saint Andrew's Cross and a spanking bench, the furniture down here is minimal. The private rooms are all kept upstairs.

I know for a fact that there's a little hallway that cuts off from the main room partially hidden behind a faux wall. It's intended to be discreet so no one gets the foolish idea to wander off that way. There's a staff bathroom down here, a tight security booth, and the emergency exit door.

As I'm crossing to that space, I snap my neck around and stare at Anita, crouched on the floor behind a low cabinet.

She gives me a sheepish grin. "Hi."

I grin back, launching myself at her. She shrieks, and thank God the tuneless Christmas music upstairs blocks that noise out. Screams can cause an issue when it isn't cries of pleasure, and I don't actually know if Callie told anyone what we were doing downstairs. If security shows to break us up, that's a definite mood killer.

My fingers drag across her calf, missing her as I land on one knee. She scrambles backwards, eyes wide with excitement as she scurries to her feet. I'm after her in an instant, and when she darts for the backdoor my grin widens.

"Run all you want, Lifeline! The longer you avoid me the harder I'll fuck you."

She gasps as she takes off down the hall, and I'm only a couple paces behind her. Adrenaline must drive her movements, because my legs are longer and I'm typically faster than she is.

"You're not getting me without a fight!" she calls back, and I watch her slam into the exit door. It flies open, spitting her out into the night, and I'm right on her heels.

There's a surprised gasp as she takes off again, and I'm sure it's the surge of cold air hitting her. It attacks my lungs, making me gasp at the temperature difference, but the click of her shoes in the dark parking lot drives me to keep moving.

We parked out here when it was still full. I halfway wonder if she'll go for the car, but quickly discard that idea. I still have the keys in my pocket, so she can't hide inside the vehicle.

I follow the click of her shoes, her breathing heavy now in the dark night. The sky is light with white clouds, but not bright enough to help my eyes adjust to keep up with her. We can run around this parking lot all night until I catch and fuck her, or we can venture off down the block. I don't particularly care where I catch her, but I will catch her.

"Come out, come out, Lifeline," I sing, jogging around the lot. It's not icy out, but a light sprinkle of snow has started to fall. I can feel it on my hands and nose, and it makes me puff out more breaths as we run. My cock is so hard it aches, and I won't be giving it to her easy when I find her.

The clicking stops, so she's hiding someplace close. I stop running, listening for her heavy breathing in the dark lot. They've turned off the parking lot lights for this, making it just a little easier for her to evade me.

I scan the area, ignoring the wind hitting my bare arms. There's maybe a dozen scattered cars out here, and I can see mine parked a good distance away.

There's the sound of slipping, and Anita curses softly from behind the nearest car. I grin again, darting around the car at the same time she gasps.

She smacks my hand when I almost grab her, taking off across the pavement. As we move I realize where she's heading, and I slide my hand into my pocket for the button with a laugh.

Anita shrieks when the alarm beeps, all doors to my ride unlocking. She dares to look back at me, nearly colliding with the car before she spins around again. The interior lights turn on for a moment, and I can hear her heavy breathing as I near her.

It just makes me think about the creek in the park, and shoving her head beneath the water...

Tonight there's no water, and as I get closer she throws open one of the backseat doors to get away. I don't know if she's just given up on reason or thinks I can't grab her in there. I have the damn key after all.

"Poor choice, Lifeline," I call to her, and she shoots me a grin. I slow my steps as I approach, waiting to see what her plan is. She's not going to outrun me, we both know it, and dashing across the parking lot only served to fog up my glasses a little. I pull them off as I approach, sliding them into my pocket before I adjust the lone earring I wear.

Her eyes track my movements as she turns in the car, her hands coming up to try and drag the door closed. I catch it before she can, and we start pulling back and forth in the space. Nobody is parked directly next to me and I rip the door open and out of her grasp as she lets out a small *oomf*.

Then I pounce, pinning her legs down with my upper body as I reach up to kill the interior lights. Anita moans before remembering to put up a fight, struggling against my body as she pushes on my face. Icy wind snaps against my back, and the idea forming in my head might make her hesitate, but I'm all for it.

Besides, she's the one that ran to the car like a safety net.

I drag her further down the seat, and she keeps beating her hands against me. One of mine slides beneath her dress, gripping the fabric of her tights, and tears straight through the weak material.

"Russell!" she gasps, eyes widening as I touch smooth skin. "I would've removed those."

"I didn't want you to remove them," I growl. "I wanted to tear them off of you."

Anita's protests turn to moans when I skim my fingers along her pussy, feeling how wet she is through the thin fabric. It would be so easy to spin her around, pin her to the seat cushion, and fuck her until I'm satisfied. But that's probably what she's expecting, and I like keeping her on her toes.

Teasing her through one side of the skimpy underwear, her body shakes at my touch. She's biting into her lip so hard to keep quiet that she's going to puncture the skin, and I grin as I feel her pussy lips for the briefest moment, watching those pretty eyes roll. My other hand feels around for my keys and hits the second button.

The trunk pops open, lifting in slow motion like it always does. It distracts Anita, who stares with wide eyes as the cabin of my ride lights up again. She's still covered, and I won't even require her to get bare for this next part.

I slide out of the SUV, grabbing her legs and dragging her with me. When she's far enough out I bend and toss her over my shoulder, enjoying the way she gasps.

"Russell-"

A quick slap on her ass has her moaning over complaining, and I haul us around to the trunk, eyeing the empty space as I turn to sit in the bed. I slide her off my shoulder before she hits her head, settling her beside me with a smirk.

"Now, Lifeline, you're going to ride me to keep me from fucking you on the hood of this car."

# 9 Anita

I stare at Russell's smirk, trying to decide if this is a joke or reality. But his hooded eyes never stray from my face, waiting for a reaction, and I suppose it's going to be a night of firsts.

Swallowing my nerves, I can't stop the thrill that rolls through my body at the idea of fucking outside again. We don't have sex outside that often because I don't like people watching. The national park was an exception, but just outside a sex club feels like we're pushing the limits.

He leans in close to me, his teeth gliding across my throat before he kisses down my jaw, speaking when he reaches my lips. "There's a reason we picked at the end. There aren't many people left inside, and most of them know to take their time leaving."

My breath hitches, my heart beating faster as I realize Russell had a hand in my gift tonight. There's no way Callie, despite her love of everyone, knew my shoe size. And these are so damn cute, I'd almost believe my loving boyfriend picked them out.

But Callie has great style.

My lips slam against his, my arms coming up to wrap around him as I slide onto his lap. Good thing this car has high ceilings, and I slide my fingers down his body to finger the outline of his cock. He's had a hard on since the stage, and I've loved watching him strain to stay in control while I hung in the air above him.

Chasing me? I knew he'd catch me, and to be honest as fun as being chased is I've waited all night to feel him inside me. I'm getting impatient, desperately needing that full feeling.

Russell's grip is firm when he slides his hand up, gripping my throat but not yet squeezing. "I've seen your face before, beautiful. I want to see you shake while you ride me."

I don't understand what he's hinting at until he starts twisting my hips, and I realize he wants me to face away and stare out into the parking lot. My cheeks burn at the idea, imagining if anyone I know saw me.

I stiffen. "Alpha."

Russell stops pushing me, releasing my throat to hold my chin. "Do you want to stop?"

I nibble my lip. "What if someone sees?"

"No one should," he replies, but that doesn't mean they won't. "If they do, no one is going to touch you without your permission. Think of it like playing with Tyson. He wouldn't do something you didn't like, and anyone who's still here isn't going to risk crossing a line and getting caught. You're safe with me, always."

It's the same thing I've heard over and over, but for some reason hearing him speak like this while we're out here makes it feel more… definite. Like I needed the confirmation of things I already know to shed that veil of uncertainty.

I slide away from his grip and turn, pressing to my hands to kick one leg over his waist. When I settle in his lap, I'm not even a little surprised to feel the warm length of his cock pressing against me skin-to-skin. Those pants he's wearing have easy access.

Reaching between us, I focus my gaze on the club. With the lights low and fresh snow beginning to fall, it looks like my home away from home encased in a holiday card. This is a place I found myself when all hope felt lost.

Russell reaches around, holding my throat again, and it silences the wayward thoughts in my head. As his cock brushes against my pussy, the underwear gets shoved aside by his other hand just before I feel him sliding inside me.

I drop my hips, shoving him deep as he groans and tightens his hand on my neck. I throw my head back, my hair brushing the space between my shoulder blades, and balance myself with one hand as I begin to rock on him.

And God, after being chased by him and teased for a few hours, having him inside me feels absolutely perfect.

"There you are," he tells me, his voice rough in one ear as I move. The hole he tore in my tights is just big enough for him to fit his cock through, and I have no doubt he'll continue to rip them to gain all the access he needs. Every single piercing down the length of his cock rubs deliciously inside me, making me whimper at the feel. At this angle he hits all the right spots, each little piercing making me feel more and more sensitive.

"You ride my cock so well, Lifeline," he grunts, shifting his hips beneath me to meet every bounce. I don't ride Russell very often, and it's been a while since I did so without the support of a suspension harness, but as he flexes his hand around my throat and grunts in my ear I can't really remember why I've denied us this. It feels so damn good.

He shoves up my dress as I ride him, planting my hands on the edge of the trunk for better leverage. Lifting the skirt he finds the tear in my tights and rips back, making me whimper as his hand palms my bare ass. He slides between the shredded material, ripping more until it reaches the waistband and tears with a sharp tug.

Then his palm lands hard on a bare cheek, my whole body jolting at the contact. I moan and pick up the pace, slapping one hand on the floor of the trunk as he plays with me. I might be on top, but I'm not in charge.

Russell grunts as he fucks his cock up into my body, making me cry out. My orgasm is approaching way too fast, and even biting my lip can't quiet the noises climbing up my throat when he swats my ass again, and again, and again.

"Cum all over me, gorgeous," he says, an air of cockiness in his voice. I've dropped my gaze to his legs, trying to keep my voice down as he traces my ass with his fingers. "Give it to me."

I can't hold back, not with all the teasing and the adrenaline pounding through me. Sliding down his cock a few more times I cry out, feeling the rush as the orgasm sweeps through me. Russell never stops, so he isn't there quite yet, and I'm hypersensitive to every thrust after my orgasm.

He gives me a beat to shake and moan on top of him, trying to keep pace with his thrusts. Then his hand on my ass slides to my hip, and he tightens his grip on my throat before tugging, pulling me back to him again.

His touch cuts off my air for a moment, making me gasp for breath at the intensity. "Now do it again for him."

My heavy eyes widen as I realize there's someone approaching, and my body wants to freeze. But Russell doesn't stop, flexing his palm along my throat again, and I dig my nails into his legs and gasp for breath. It only works to make him move faster, and my brain can't decide if I love or hate that.

All my fears of being caught melt when I recognize the figure approaching us. He's wearing a winter jacket so I can't see most of his piercings, save for the septum piercing and the one through his eyebrow that catches the light.

Tyson's green-hazel eyes twinkle in the lights of Russell's car. He stops walking, the snow creating a light layer across his shoulders. His lip hooks up into a smirk, and he looks so unsurprised to find Russell with his cock inside me out here I can't help wondering if they planned this.

He smirks at us, and Russell starts fucking me a little harder so I gasp. "You two are having fun."

Russell's fingers flex on my throat, and I almost lose it all over again. "Answer him, Lifeline."

"Yes," I moan.

Tyson nods, his hand coming out for a moment to trace my chin. Russell might be a sharer, but I know there's lines you aren't supposed to cross when it comes to respect. Right now my brain is too scrambled to figure out if this crosses any.

But my alpha-male doesn't seem concerned, leaving a wet kiss on my neck right where his fingers end. "Still don't want to join?"

That piques my interest. I haven't had the pleasure of playing with Tyson for a while. But he just smirks and shakes his head, winking at us. "I have mine waiting at home."

Russell nods, and when Tyson's fingers brush over my lips I can't stop the second orgasm. I cum with a cry, one that Russell fucks me through.

The sensation makes my eyes roll, and Tyson's hand leaves my skin. When I blink my eyes open, he's gone, and Russell is grunting behind me.

He moves to slide me off and I assist, slamming my hands down once more in front of me. His cock slides free seconds before I feel him covering my ass with cum, my head falling forward as I try to catch my breath.

There's a moment of silence, then Russell is helping me shift around as he covers me with the dress. I'm a mess, but short of going inside to clean up I'll be using the dress and perhaps his coat until we get back home.

When he's no longer beneath me, he holds my face tenderly and gives me a long kiss. "You did so good."

I sigh against his lips, lingering for a moment longer before pulling back. His molten eyes find mine, and for a moment neither of us moves. Sometime during the run his blond locks got disheveled, and he looks like he's been standing in the wind instead of fucking me inside the car. I reach up and run my fingers through it, messing up the waves even more.

He chuckles, brushing his thumb across my cheek. "Are you ready to go home, Lifeline?"

I take a breath, eyeing the sky. The white clouds look even fluffier than before, but I know it's pretty late. Now that we aren't busy with each other I realize my fingers are cold, and my face feels cool too. I lick my chapped lips before looking at him again. "Is it time to decorate?"

Russell scoffs, but there's a hidden smile beneath it. He slides out of the trunk and helps me out before tapping a button to release the door. It begins to close, and I peer around, but Tyson is already out of sight.

His arms come around me, the falling snow dusting his face. "You want to decorate at midnight?"

"It's a great way to kick off tomorrow."

He chuckles low in his throat, leaning in to brush his nose against mine. "The only thing I'm going to decorate at this hour, Lifeline, is you. If you'll let me string you up, I'll wrap you in all the tinsel and lights you can handle."

A laugh escapes me at the idea, at the same time that a rush sweeps through me. The idea doesn't sound bad, and Russell is so very good at ties…

I stand on my toes, kissing his lips once more. The flurry of snow invites in the cheer of the holidays that I hold close, and when our foreheads press together it's the romantic moment I've always dreamed of. "Then you better take me home."

## Ready to see what happens when Tyson meets Kat?

Games of Temptation
2025

## See what drew Jo and Vinny away from the club, in their upcoming spinoff:

What's Left of Me (book 1)
2025

Printed in Dunstable, United Kingdom